Can You Top That?

W. Nikola-Lisa

illustrated by Hector Viveros Lee

Lee & Low Books Inc. · New York

Printed in Hong Kong by South China Printing Co. (1988) Ltd.

Book design by Tania Garcia
Book production by The Kids at Our House

The text is set in Goudy.
The illustrations are rendered in gouache, India ink, and
watercolor using a wash-off technique. First, a pencil drawing of the
image is made on illustration board and white gouache is applied in the
areas made by the drawing. After the paint dries, black India ink is
brushed quickly over the entire board surface, saturating the penciled
areas not protected by the gouache. Once the ink is dry, the board is
washed off, leaving a faux woodcut drawing. The image is transferred
onto acetate film and also onto a clean illustration board, where it is
painted with watercolor and gouache. In some images pastel chalk was
also used. The acetate is then placed over the painting.

10 9 8 7 6 5 4 3 2 1
First Edition

Library of Congress Cataloging-in-Publication Data
Nikola-Lisa, W.
    Can you top that? / by W. Nikola-Lisa ; illustrated by Hector
Viveros Lee.— 1st ed.
        p. cm.
    Summary: Children drawing animals on the ground at the
park compete to see who has the most impressive one, from a
fish with one fin to a horse with ten heads.
    ISBN 1-880000-99-7
    [1. Animals—Fiction. 2. Drawing—Fiction. 3. Counting.]
I. Lee, Hector Viveros, ill. II. Title.
PZ7.N5855 Can 2000
[E]—dc21
                                        99-047895

To Callie, Megan, and Spirit—RUFF! —W.N.-L.

To my grandparents, in whose arms is the smell of home. —H.V.L.

A fish
with one fin—
I got a mouse
with two tails!

Can you top that?

Can you top that?

A snake
with **three** tongues—
I got a **bird**
with **four** wings!

Can you top that?

A cat
with five eyes—
I got a dog
with six ears!

A dog
with **six** ears—
I got a **pig**
with **seven** snouts!

Can you **top** that?

A pig
with seven snouts—
I got a goat
with eight horns!

A goat
with **eight** horns—
I got a **cow**
with **nine** legs!

A cow
with nine legs—
I got a horse
with ten heads!

Can you top that?

A horse
with **ten** heads—
Why that ain't nothing.
I got an elephant!

An elephant?

Yeah, an elephant!

Well, what's so special
'bout an elephant?

You got one?

Well, ah, no . . .
But, hey,
can we see it?

Sure, just as soon
as you show me . . .
a horse with ten heads,
a cow with nine legs,
a goat with eight horns,
a pig with seven snouts,
a dog with six ears,
a cat with five eyes,
a bird with four wings,
a snake with three tongues,
a mouse with two tails,
and a fish with one fin!

Ah, man—
you're no fun!